For Jane
Thank you for all your encouragement.

Printed in Mexico
This book is set in 30-pt. Kennerley.
First Edition
1 3 5 7 9 10 8 6 4 2

Library of Congress Cataloging-in-Publication Data
Morgan-Vanroyen, Mary, 1957-
Curious Rosie/ Mary Morgan—1st ed.
p. cm.
Summary: A little mouse is curious about everything, including what snowflakes taste like, how a clock
works, and what happens when she blows on a dandelion.
ISBN 0-7868-0477-7 (trade)
[1. Mice—Fiction. 2. Curiosity—Fiction.] I. Title.
PZ7.V353Cu 2000
[E]—dc21 99-20983

Visit www.hyperionchildrensbooks.com,
part of the GO Network

Curious
ROSIE

MARY MORGAN

HYPERION BOOKS FOR CHILDREN

NEW YORK

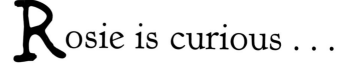

Rosie is curious . . .

about many things.

She wonders what
snowflakes taste like,

and how the clock works.

Rosie wonders who lives
in the little hill . . .

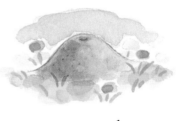

ants!

Rosie wonders what's
in the jar,

and what will happen when
she blows on a dandelion.

Rosie wonders, "Who's that?

It's baby Rosie!